Starry Forest Books, Inc. • P.O. Box 1797, 217 East 70th Street, New York, NY 10021 • Starry Forest® is a registered trademark of Starry Forest Books, Inc. • Text and Illustrations © 2019 by Starry Forest Books, Inc. • This 2019 edition published by Starry Forest Books, Inc. • All rights reserved. No part of this publication may be reproduced, stored in a retrieval system, or transmitted in any form or by any means (including electronic, mechanical, photocopying, recording, or otherwise) without prior written permission from the publisher. • ISBN 978-1-946260-33-8 • Manufactured in Huizhou City, Guangdong Province, China • Lot #: 2 4 6 8 10 9 7 5 3 1 • 04/19

CLASSIC STORIES

Greek Myths

retold by
Caroline Hickey

illustrated by
Teresa Martinez

Starry Forest Books

PEGASUS

HERCULES

THE TROJAN HORSE

PEGASUS

Once there was a beautiful horse named Pegasus. His coat was pure white. His mane and tail were as fine as silk. His heart was brave and strong. Pegasus was no ordinary horse – he could fly. His huge, powerful wings lifted him, swift and sure, into the sky.

Athena, Goddess of Wisdom, loved Pegasus. She protected him and made sure that he was well fed and cared for. Pegasus enjoyed happy, carefree days, soaring over mountains and galloping through the clouds.

One day, a warrior named Bellerophon fell in love with a clever princess named Philonoe. But her father, King Jobates, had been ordered by another king to kill Bellerophon. King Jobates didn't know what to do. He was fond of Bellerophon, but he couldn't ignore the other king's command.

    King Jobates had an idea. A ferocious monster called a Chimera was attacking his kingdom. The Chimera had the head of a lion, the body of a goat, and the scales, claws, and wings of a dragon. Night after night, it swooped down, spewing flames, grabbing up animals and terrifying the people.

    "Kill the Chimera," King Jobates told Bellerophon, "and you may wed Philonoe."

"You can defeat the Chimera if you ride Pegasus," Philonoe told Bellerophon. "Ask Athena for help."

So Bellerophon prayed to Athena. Athena gave him a golden bridle and told him he would find Pegasus at a spring.

With a rush of wings, Pegasus landed. He recognized the bridle, and knew he could trust Bellerophon.

"We must find the Chimera," Bellerophon said, "and kill it." With one mighty flap of his wings, Pegasus launched them into the sky. They tracked the Chimera to its cave by following its gray trail of smoke.

The Chimera emerged from the cave, roaring. Pegasus beat back the beast with his powerful hooves and Bellerophon tried again and again to spear the Chimera.

    Then in a burst of strength, Pegasus shot forward so Bellerophon could plunge his spear into the Chimera's heart. With a deafening howl, the Chimera fell dead.

King Jobates kept his promise, and happy Bellerophon and Philonoe were soon wed. Everyone in the kingdom came to cheer the loving couple and to thank Pegasus.

Pegasus joined Athena on Mount Olympus where he lived happily and peacefully the rest of his days.

HERCULES

Hercules was famous for being strong. But he was determined to prove that he was heroic. He especially wanted his father, Zeus, the most powerful of all the gods, to respect him.

"Perform these Twelve Impossible Tasks," said King Eurystheus, "and you will prove that you are a hero."

"I'll do all twelve," promised Hercules.

It took ten years for Hercules to complete the first ten tasks. He conquered a lion and a nine-headed snake. He captured a boar, a bear, a bull, birds, cattle, and horses. He cleaned stables and stole a goddess's sash. But the eleventh task — stealing golden apples that belonged to the Goddess Hera — was the hardest yet.

Hera, queen of the gods, kept her apples in a garden at the edge of the world. Fearless nymphs guarded the apples with the help of a hundred-headed dragon. They drove Hercules away again and again.

Not far from the garden, Hercules killed an eagle that was pecking a man to pieces.

"I owe you my life," said the man. "May I help you in some way?"

Hercules explained about the apples for King Eurystheus.

"Find Atlas, who holds up the world," said the man. "He can get the apples for you. The nymphs will gladly give him some, because they are his daughters."

Hercules said to Atlas, "I will hold the world while you get the apples." Atlas agreed. But when he returned, he said slyly, "Let me bring the apples to the king for you."

"Very well," said Hercules. "Please just hold the world for a moment while I put padding on my shoulders."

Atlas put the apples on the ground and took the world back onto his shoulders.

Hercules picked up the apples. "You tricked me," he said to Atlas. "Now I'll trick you." He ran off as fast as he could, leaving Atlas howling in anger.

Proud Hercules delivered the golden apples to King Eurystheus.

"How did you get these?" asked the king. "No one – not even Zeus – has ever done so before."

"I'll explain someday," said Hercules, smiling. "But now I must go." And with that, Hercules set off to complete his twelfth and final task: capturing Cerberus, the three-headed dog with a serpent tail who guarded the gates of the underworld.

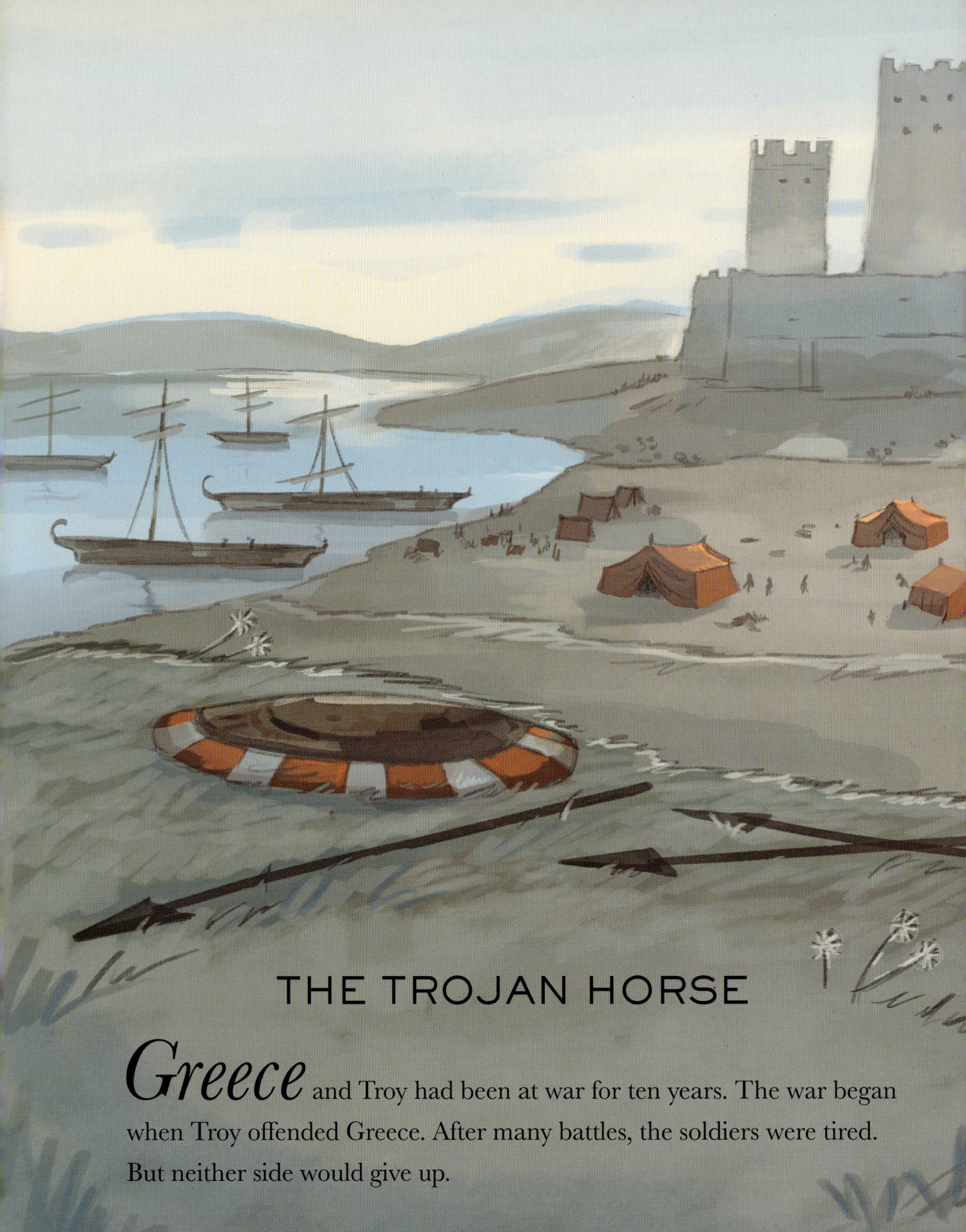

THE TROJAN HORSE

Greece and Troy had been at war for ten years. The war began when Troy offended Greece. After many battles, the soldiers were tired. But neither side would give up.

The city of Troy was surrounded by a wall so high it seemed to block out the sky. The Trojan people were safe behind the wall. Again and again, the Greeks battled to break through. But the Trojans stood on top of the wall and rained down arrows, rocks, and spears on the Greeks. The Greeks would retreat, regroup, and attack again.

Odysseus led the Greek army. After yet another defeat, he summoned the generals.

"Let's dig a tunnel under the wall," suggested one.

"Let's circle the wall and attack from all sides at once," said a second.

"Let's burn the wall down," said a third.

Odysseus spoke at last. "I'm weary of war and seeing my soldiers die. I long for home. We can't defeat the Trojans by force. We have to outsmart them."

The Trojans awoke one morning to see that the Greeks had sailed away. They left only the ruins of their camp – and an enormous wooden horse. "The Greeks have left us a gift to honor our victory," boasted the Trojan generals. "Open the gate! Wheel the horse inside!"

The Trojans cheered. They wheeled the giant horse inside the city gates, and celebrated all day and well into the night.

The Trojans did not know that the horse was hollow. As they slept after their celebration, Greek soldiers hidden in the horse's belly slid open a trapdoor, and crept out.

Silently, they opened the city gate and let in the rest of the Greek army that had been hiding nearby.

Once the Greek soldiers were inside the city, they quickly defeated the Trojans, who were completely unprepared. The Trojans surrendered.

The Greeks didn't stop to revel in their triumph, though. Odysseus spoke for all of the soldiers when he said, "Peace is our victory. Come, let us now go home."